THE HAUNTING OF HILLSIDE SCHOOL

by Kristiana Gregory

SCHOLASTIC INC.
New York   Toronto   London   Auckland   Sydney
Mexico City   New Delhi   Hong Kong   Buenos Aires

If you purchased this book without a cover, you should be aware that this
book is stolen property. It was reported as "unsold and destroyed" to the
publisher, and neither the author nor the publisher has received any
payment for this "stripped book."

No part of this publication may be reproduced, stored
in a retrieval system, or transmitted in any form or by any means,
electronic, mechanical, photocopying, recording, or otherwise, without
written permission of the publisher. For information regarding permission,
write to Scholastic Inc., Attention: Permissions Department, 557 Broadway,
New York, NY 10012.

ISBN-13: 978-0-545-00378-0
ISBN-10: 0-545-00378-4

Text copyright © 2008 by Kristiana Gregory.
All rights reserved. Published by Scholastic Inc.

SCHOLASTIC, LITTLE APPLE, and associated logos are trademarks
and/or registered trademarks of Scholastic Inc.

12 11 10 9   10 11 12 13/0

Printed in the U.S.A.   40

First printing, September 2008

CHAPTERS

For Dylan, Christopher, and Matthew Gregory

1

"Something's Out There"

The old schoolhouse creaked in the autumn wind. Nine-year-old Claire Posey was upstairs in her after-school pottery class when suddenly she turned to look out the window. A girl's face, pale and round, was staring in. But how could that be? The art room was high up on the second floor.

As Claire blinked, the face disappeared. Stunned, she blinked again, but all she saw were the mountains and stormy sky. When a sharp gust of wind rattled the windowpane, she rubbed her arms, shivering.

"*David*," she whispered to her cousin, who was beside her at the table.

"Just a second." David Bridger was ten years old and busy shaping a submarine out of his clay. Rows of miniature torpedoes covered his math book. His blond hair hung over his eyes.

"David, something's out there. A girl. She was looking in at us."

"What?" He jumped up, knocking his chair to the floor.

Hands sticky with clay, the cousins dashed to the window, followed by several other students who had heard the commotion. They all peered out. Two stories below, the ground was carpeted with golden leaves.

"Weird," said Claire. "There's no ladder or anything."

"Maybe someone climbed this tree," David said. He wiped his hands on his shirt, looking out at a tall aspen. Its branches were nearly bare, its remaining leaves fluttering in the wind. Two squirrels were chasing each other down its trunk, but there was no girl.

"She had dark hair, in two braids," Claire said.

Ronald McCoy pressed his goopy hands to the glass, then smooshed the clay around, creating a mess. He was Claire's age. "So what d'you see now?" he said to her. "A ghost? *Whooo, whooo*, I'm so scared. In the olden days, a girl got murdered here, so maybe she's haunting this place —"

"Boys and girls!" called Miss Wiggins, clapping her hands for their attention. She was their art instructor and also taught ballet on Saturdays. "Return to your seats, please, and tidy up. Ronald McCoy, once again you'll be staying after class, this time to clean that window."

Claire and David wiped off their table and washed up at the sink. Long ago, Hillside School had been a mansion, and this room had been a butler's kitchen. The town of Cabin Creek was so small, and the mansion was so big, all the children from kindergarten through ninth grade were able to attend Hillside.

"Claire, let's get Jeff. Maybe he saw something, too," David said, referring to his older brother, who was downstairs at his guitar lesson. "Ready?"

"Yep," said Claire. Being practical and in a hurry, she dried her hands on the seat of her jeans instead of using a paper towel. She hefted her backpack to her shoulder. Her curly red hair was in a ponytail, which bounced as they rushed down the wide staircase. Jeff was waiting for them in the entry hall, neatly dressed in a sweater and collared shirt. When they told him what had happened, his brown eyes sparkled with mischief. He was twelve and always ready for adventure.

"A ghost? *Really?*" Jeff grinned. He picked up his guitar case. "Okay, then. We better start investigating."

The schoolhouse cast a long shadow in the late afternoon. The cousins searched the bushes for a ladder or a scaffold. They tried finding footholds in the large stones of the building — to see if someone could have climbed up — but the cracks were too narrow. And the tree's branches weren't close enough to the second-floor window for anyone to have perched.

Gazing up, they noticed a light in the art room. Ronald McCoy was cleaning the glass. When he looked down and saw the cousins, he stuck out his tongue at them.

"That window's pretty high up," Jeff said, giving Ronald a friendly wave.

"And there're no climbing ropes or pulleys," added David. "Claire, are you sure —?"

"Guys, I know what I saw! It was a girl with braids. Dark hair. She was watching us." Claire zipped up her sweatshirt, stomping her feet to keep warm. Prepared as usual, she pulled mittens from her pocket and put them on.

The air was growing cold. The aspen and oak trees were swishing in the wind. Leaves swirled across the lawn with a noisy crackle.

Jeff looked up at the storm clouds. "Guys, let's go home. Something's giving me the creeps."

2

The Terrible Tragedy

The cousins coasted their bikes down the hill from school, Jeff's guitar tied to the rack on his rear fender. Town was so close that they reached the Western Café without having to pedal. They said hello to Aunt Lilly and Uncle Wyatt, Claire's parents, who were the café owners and often worked during the dinner hours. Next, the kids rode to the animal hospital, where the boys' mother, Dr. Daisy Bridger, was the veterinarian.

Not wanting to worry their parents, they didn't mention the mysterious face Claire had seen. However, as soon as they reached the trail that cut through the woods, they rode as fast as they could. Black clouds were bunched up over the mountains. Riding into the wind, the cousins kept glancing behind them, toward their school on the hill.

"What if it *was* a ghost?" David cried as their wheels crunched over twigs and pine needles. He had forgotten his sweater again and was shivering.

"I don't believe in ghosts!" Claire yelled.

"Then why're we riding so fast?" Jeff asked.

"Just in case!" cried David. "Plus, it's freezing out here!"

Soon the trail opened up to the sandy beach

where their log homes faced the lake. For miles around there was only forest and shore-line and the secluded Lost Island. No one else lived this far out except their trusted family friend, Mr. Wellback. His cabin was up a twisty road that also looked out over the lake.

The old man greeted them at the boys' kitchen door, a dish towel over his shoulder. He wore a chef's apron that matched his white hair and white beard.

"Your folks are working late," Mr. Wellback told the kids as they petted their woofing and wiggling dogs. "I'm here to make sure you lolly-gaggers get your supper and to help with homework."

There was a fire in the fireplace and the cabin smelled good from spaghetti and garlic bread. David set the table while Jeff put out bottles of salad dressing. Claire poured four glasses of water. Then they fed their pets. There was old Tessie the yellow Lab, Rascal the Scottish terrier, and Yum-Yum, Claire's little white poodle with a sparkly pink collar.

Finally, everyone was seated. Mr. Wellback said a blessing, then tucked a napkin under his chin. "So what did you rabble-rousers do today?"

The cousins looked at one another. They shifted uneasily in their chairs.

"Have I ever spilled the beans?" Mr. Wellback asked them.

"Never," Claire said.

"Well, then, out with it. What happened?"

"Hillside School is haunted!" David said.

"Haunted? Hmm." The old man sprinkled Parmesan cheese on his spaghetti, then on his

salad, then on his bread. "Hmm," he said again. "Go on."

When Claire explained about the murdered girl from the olden days, Mr. Wellback set his fork down. "I've lived here all my life and never heard *that* whopper. But then, there *was* that terrible tragedy. Two, actually."

"What? What?" they wanted to know. They called their friend Mr. Wellback because of the way he started his stories.

The old man wiped his beard. "Well, back in the year 1918, Hillside wasn't a school yet. It was a mansion owned by the wealthy Tuttle family. Seven sons and a little daughter named Nettie. She was adored by all."

Mr. Wellback paused at the sound of rain splattering the windows. Coals in the fireplace hissed from wind in the chimney.

Hearing the storm, the cousins scooted closer to one another for comfort.

"As you might imagine," he continued, "with all those brothers, Nettie was a tomboy. But she also loved to dance and draw and play the piano. When an influenza epidemic swept the country —"

Claire raised her hand.

"You're interrupting me, young lady."

"I'm sorry, but what's an *in . . . flu . . . enza*?"

"A virus," he answered. "The flu. At first, Nettie's parents thought she was just chilled from swimming out at Lost Island with her brothers, even though it was summer. But at sundown, her shivers had turned to pneumonia. By midnight, when the doctor arrived in his carriage, Nettie was dead, poor thing. Just nine years old. The pandemic was quick and dreadful. That means people all over the world died."

Jeff began cutting slices of chocolate cake and handing out spoons. David scooped ice cream. It was their traditional dessert with Mr. Wellback. They were silent so he would keep telling his story. Claire set a heaping plate in front of him.

"Anyhow," he went on, "Mr. and Mrs. Tuttle were so heartbroken and worried their sons would also perish — the oldest boy was only fifteen years old — well, the family moved away from Cabin Creek. To honor Nettie's memory, they donated their mansion to the town, to be used for a school. Peculiar folks. They insisted Nettie's attic bedroom stay exactly as it had been while she was alive. When I was a boy in class, we thought we heard piano music coming from behind those locked doors. But no one had been up there for years and years. Spooked us good. Now and then, we'd see an odd little man hurrying through the woods behind school. Always carried a small sack, but who he was or what he was doing, we never found out. You scallywags probably don't know there's a secret passage-way to the attic."

Their spoons stopped midair. "Secret passageway?"

"That's right. One of my classmates got lost in there. By the time they found the poor lad, he'd been dead a whole day. He had fallen through some rotten wood and landed in the basement."

3

A Sound from Nowhere

The next day was Friday, which meant that after school, the cousins went to their painting class together. They all got to work on projects to sell at the school's fundraiser. They kept an eye on the window, but no face appeared.

When the hour was up, they rinsed their brushes in the sink. Suddenly, Claire looked toward the door. She looked around her. Then she looked up at the ceiling.

"Guys? What's that sound?"

Jeff turned off the squeaky faucet. David stood still. Soon they heard the delicate notes of a piano. The music seemed to be echoing through a heater grate in the wooden floor.

"Miss Wiggins?" Claire asked, waving her hand in the air. "Miss Wiggins, where is that music coming from?"

The teacher cocked her head, listening. "I imagine from the other wing of the school," she answered. She closed her eyes, smiling. "Mm. Lovely. Mozart's Minuet in D Major. But someone must be playing a CD. There are no pianos at Hillside School."

"No pianos?" The cousins glanced at one another.

"That's right," she replied. "We haven't had

the money to replace the one ruined in a storm. Our leaky roof gets worse every year."

In the hallway, the cousins whispered. "There's a piano *somewhere*," said Claire.

Jeff agreed. "Whoever is playing keeps stopping to repeat notes, like they're learning a new chord or something. I do that on my guitar. It's definitely *not* a CD."

"What if it *is* Nettie's ghost?" David asked. "Remember how Mr. Wellback said he heard stuff when he was a kid?"

"*Yeah*," said his older brother. "It's weird all right. Come on, guys, let's see what we can find."

The cousins stayed close together as they

explored the halls. They kept stopping to listen for the piano. Hillside School was shaped like a giant *U*. After-school music and dance classes were down one wing, art and drama down the other. Many rooms upstairs in the Tuttle mansion had been divided into smaller ones. This was so children could have quiet little areas to draw, dance, or practice their musical instruments. A window in every door allowed the teachers to check on their students from the hallway.

Down the music wing, violins and flutes sounded like an orchestra warming up before a concert. In one of the rooms, a boy was playing scales on his trumpet. Next door to him was a clarinet.

"French horn over here," announced Jeff.

"Guitar," David reported from the other side of the hall.

Claire jumped on her toes to see in a window. "Oboe!" she said.

When they turned a corner, they could hear the Mozart minuet loud and clear.

"It's coming from Room Twelve," cried David, "but there's no window."

Jeff said, "I hear it, too."

Claire turned the knob. The bottom of the door was so warped, it scraped against the floor. It moved only an inch. For a moment the piano music continued, then fell silent. The cousins froze. They waited and listened. They pushed the door open another inch, then another. Finally, they were able to squeeze through.

The room was dark except for a high, round window. Cobwebs wobbled from the ceiling.

Dust motes floated in a ray of afternoon sunlight.

"Hello?" they said. "Anyone here?" They took their flashlights from their packs and flicked them on. Before them was a jumble of old wooden desks, chairs, and chalkboards.

"Hello?" they called again.

But the only sound was the creaking of floorboards as they crept among the shadowy furniture.

Then they saw the piano. It was an upright, dark with water stains. Its keyboard sagged. A wooden stool was covered in dust.

Jeff tapped his fingers over the black keys, then the white ones. The notes plunked and clunked, like spoons on a tin can. "No one could've played Mozart on this old thing," he said. "It's way out of tune."

"And look at this stool," said Claire. She drew a smiley face in the dust. "No one has sat here in a million years."

David shook his head. "I don't get it. *Someone* was in here. We heard the music." He unzipped his backpack again, this time for his notebook. Quickly he drew the piano. Then he flipped to another page and sketched the cobwebs and round window. He was in the habit of drawing clues whenever they investigated a mystery.

Jeff lifted his head. He sniffed the air. Claire did the same, then David. They glanced around the room with worried looks. They sniffed and sniffed. An aroma of cinnamon filled the room.

"What's it coming from?"

"Whatever it is," said Jeff, "I think we should get out of here as fast as we can."

4

Bad News

The cousins hurried out of the dusty storage room. But the instant they dragged the door shut — with a *slam!* — the piano music started up again. And the strange odor grew stronger. The children looked at one another with wide eyes.

In a trembling voice, David said, "Do ghosts smell like gingerbread . . . or cinnamon?"

"I don't believe in ghosts!" Claire reminded them as she backed away from the door.

"Me, neither," said Jeff.

They broke into a run. They ran down the hall, around the corner, and downstairs. When they reached their lockers, they were out of breath.

"Should we tell one of our teachers?" Claire asked the brothers. Her heart was still racing.

"They won't believe us."

"Maybe the spice is from something they're baking," Claire suggested. "Let's look in their lounge."

David was still holding his sketch pad. "But what does *that* have to do with the music?"

"It's spooky all right," said Jeff. "Oh, good, here we are."

The teachers' lounge had a faded couch and some chairs. There was a small refrigerator, but no stove, and the microwave was empty.

Miss Wiggins was sitting at a table, finishing a sandwich. She crumbled the wrapper into her brown lunch bag.

"Hello there," she said to the children.

"Are you having a party?" David asked.

The woman gave them a puzzled look. "I'm waiting for my sister to pick me up. What're you three up to?"

"We smelled a cake or something baking," Jeff said.

"Not at Hillside School," the teacher answered. "I'm afraid this place is so run-down, the fire department made us cancel our Junior Chef cooking classes. It's a real shame. We just don't have money to fix the ovens."

From the street out front, a horn beeped

twice. "Oh, there's my ride," Miss Wiggins said, putting on her coat. "Have a nice weekend, children. See you Monday."

The next morning, Jeff and David helped Claire rake leaves at her cabin. Then they rode their bikes to town, leaving Rascal home to keep old Tessie company. Yum-Yum was bundled in the basket on Claire's handlebars, warm in a little blue sweater that matched Claire's.

They liked exploring town on Saturdays.

First they went to the bakery and each bought an oatmeal cookie and a small carton of chocolate milk. They sat out front in the sunshine where they could see the lake. Nearby were two men in business suits, drinking coffee with their pastries.

"It'll be a great site for vacation condos," one said to the other. "It has a view of the lake and the mountains."

The other man nodded. "Can't wait till we own the land and can tear down the school. We'll make a fortune off all the tourists."

The cousins couldn't help overhearing their conversation. "Excuse me," Jeff said. "Are you talking about *Hillside* School?"

"Indeed we are. Are you students?"

"Yes. But what do you mean about turning it into condos?"

"Progress is finally coming to this town. Soon all the Cabin Creek kids will transfer to that big school in Fairfield —"

"Fairfield!" Jeff exclaimed. "It's miles away."

"Don't worry. The bus will have a DVD player to pass the time. Pretty exciting, huh?"

"No, sir, it's not exciting. Not one bit." Jeff crossed his arms, trying to stay calm. His brown hair was brushed neatly and his sweatshirt was clean. David, however, was wearing his clothes from yesterday and had misplaced his comb. He was disorganized, but he knew what he wanted to say.

"We like riding our bikes from home," the younger boy explained. "We're free as birds."

"That's right," said Claire. "Hillside is close to town where our parents work. We visit them after school. The only time we like riding a bus is when we visit Grandma and Grandpa." She hugged Yum-Yum to her chest, remembering how she missed them.

"Is that so?" The man's face turned red. He glared at the cousins. "Well, times are changing. Besides, that crummy old mansion is haunted. The sooner we tear it down, the better."

5

Strange Clues

Yum-Yum growled at two boys who had come out of the bakery. One carried a bag of donuts, and the other had a rubber band stretched between his fingers and aimed at the poodle.

"Cut it out, Ronald!" Claire said, pushing away his hand. "Yum-Yum remembers you from last time."

Ronald McCoy was with his older brother

Rex, a ninth-grader. They had heard the man say Hillside School was haunted.

"It's that girl's ghost," said Ronald. "Told you so."

Rex bit into a jelly donut. With his mouth full he said, "S'about time we get a new school. Fairfield's awesome."

"Says who?" Jeff wanted to know.

The McCoy brothers grinned at each other. Ronald shot his rubber band at a parking meter, then answered: "Our uncle works there. They have vending machines in the hallways. Plenty of sodas and candy bars any time you want. All the kids are cool."

Rex laughed, spewing bits of jelly. "And the best part," he said, "s'that there's no homework."

"No homework?" Jeff and David gave cautious smiles.

"You heard me," Rex replied. "*Nooo* homework. That's the school for me."

Without saying good-bye, the McCoys jaywalked across the street.

"What if it's true?" Claire asked her cousins.

"A school with no homework? Yes!" Jeff and David gave each other high fives.

"No!" cried Claire. "I mean, what if our school is haunted?"

"Oh," said the boys.

"Come on, guys. What if there really is a ghost? Maybe Nettie Tuttle is trying to keep the mansion from being turned into condos. That's why all this weird stuff is happening."

David suddenly rummaged through his pack. He took out his sketchbook. "I just remembered something. Look!" He showed them his drawing of the storage room. Beneath the cobwebs, he had sketched a framed portrait, partly hidden behind a tall grandfather clock.

"It was dark so I didn't get a good look," David went on, "but I think this was a painting of an old-fashioned girl."

Claire's mouth dropped open. "An old-fashioned girl? What if it's the girl I saw staring in the window?"

"Let's go back for another look!" said Jeff.

"No way." Claire shook her head. "That room freaked me out."

As Jeff gathered their chocolate milk

cartons to throw in the trash, he had another idea. "Let's go to the library."

"What for?" asked David. "I mean, I love the library, but our books aren't due till next week."

"Remember those newspapers from the old days?" Jeff said. "Maybe we'll find a picture of Nettie Tuttle —"

"— and find more clues!" Claire cried. She jumped up and carried Yum-Yum to her bike, tucking the little dog into her basket.

The library faced the park, the hardware store, and a new antique shop. The cousins sat at a window table with a stack of *Cabin Creek Gazette* issues from 1918. These were actually photocopies from the old newspapers, bound in large books. Jeff and David turned the pages in one volume, reading about airplanes during World War I.

"Check out this bomber," Jeff said. "It looks ancient."

"Yeah, cool." David was busy sketching a soldier's uniform with a round helmet.

"Hey, listen to this," Claire interrupted. She started reading: "*After Nettie Tuttle's funeral, the attic was sealed off so her bedroom would be undisturbed forever. Then the good ladies of Cabin Creek hosted a reception at the Blue Mountain Lodge. To honor the little girl's memory, the ladies served what had been her favorite dessert.* Guess what it was, guys?"

"What?"

"Spicy Gingerbread Men with Cinnamon

Buttons! Get it? *Spicy . . . Cinnamon*. Do you think that's what we smelled yesterday at school, when we heard the piano music?"

Jeff thought a moment. "This is too weird. Hey, David, could you write down these clues so we can keep 'em straight? Number One: a face in the window, but no one was there. Number Two: piano music in Room Twelve, but the piano is wrecked and the stool is dusty. No one could've sat there playing a Mozart minuet."

"Number Three," David wrote. "Spicy smell . . . like baking cake . . . but no kitchen."

"Number Four," said Claire. "Spicy gingerbread men were Nellie's favorite treat."

"So now what?" they asked one another.

They gazed out at the park. Most of the trees were bare, except for the blue spruce where they had left their bikes. Yum-Yum was sitting up in Claire's basket, ears alert. In her sweater and sparkly collar, she looked ready for action.

Claire took a deep breath. "Okay, guys, I've changed my mind. As long as Yum-Yum comes with us, we can go back to that creepy room. I want to see that old-fashioned girl in the painting."

6

A Change in Plans

When the cousins got on their bikes, they noticed a blue pickup truck pulling into the library parking lot. CABIN CREEK ANIMAL HOSPITAL was painted on the driver's door. Dr. Daisy Bridger was waving from behind the wheel, her long blond braid over her shoulder.

"There you are!" she called, smiling. "I saw your bikes."

"Hi, Mom!" said David.

"Everything okay?" asked Jeff.

"Everything's fine," she answered. "Put your bikes in back, then hop in up here with me. I need your help at home. Another storm's coming tonight. Maybe snow this time. We need to bring in firewood and finish raking before the leaves freeze to the ground. It's still sunny, so we have plenty of time."

"Okay, Mom." Jeff and David tried not to show their disappointment. They would much rather explore their haunted school with Claire, not go home and do chores. But last winter when their father was killed in an avalanche — he had been a forest ranger — the boys had promised each other that they would help their mother without complaining. At least, they would try.

As the truck turned up the gravel road to

their cabins, Dr. Bridger's pager started beeping. She glanced at it. "Uh-oh," she said. "Sorry, kids, but I've got to get back. Emergency. Listen, at five o'clock, Uncle Wyatt will pick you up so we can all have supper together at the café. Bring your dogs. Aunt Lilly said they can have the couch in the office all to themselves. Bye now, darlings. Thanks for your help. See you soon."

Jeff pushed the wheelbarrow onto the porch with their last load of firewood. The logs were stacked under the wide eaves, where they would stay dry.

"That should do it, don't you think?"

"Looks good," Claire and David agreed.

The cousins stared at the pile of leaves they had started raking several days ago, then looked out at the lake. Their red canoe was tied up at the dock, bobbing in the small waves.

"Sure is a pretty day," Jeff said. "This might be our last chance to go out to Lost Island before it snows."

"I'll get the life vests," David said.

Claire grabbed their backpacks from the porch. They began calling out their checklist:

"Walkie-talkies and whistles!"

"Canteens!"

"Binoculars!"

"First-aid kit!"

"Chocolate bars!"

"Okay, let's go!"

All summer, the three children had paddled to and from the island with their dogs. So it took only a moment before they were on their way across the bumpy lake, water sloshing against the hull. Lost Island loomed ahead. Its forest hid the path to their secret clubhouse.

As soon as they glided into the cove, the dogs jumped out and splashed to shore. The kids dragged the canoe onto the beach so it wouldn't float away, then set off through the woods. They hiked along a spongy trail of leaves — crimson, yellow, and pink.

"Fort Grizzly Paw!" they cried when they came upon the ancient log cabin. They had replaced a crumbled wall with a picket fence. It had a little gate, which they used as their entrance.

Inside, a pine tree had rooted itself in the dirt floor and was growing up through the roof. Its low branches served as a clothes rack, and knotholes in the trunk made perfect cubbies for storing Band-Aids and packs of gum. A stone fireplace was full of twigs and pinecones that had dropped into the chimney from other trees. After inspecting the dirt for footprints, the children agreed only squirrels and raccoons had been in their fort.

"Guess everything'll be safe till spring," Jeff declared.

"So, lookout tower, here we come!" cried Claire. She led her cousins to the tall oak where they had built a pulley system for delivering snacks. A platform was up top. As they climbed the bare limbs, they could see the huge lake and surrounding wilderness. With their binoculars they surveyed the town and the Marina, where most of the boats had been put into storage. Chairlifts on the ski hill dangled over brown slopes not yet covered with snow.

All of a sudden, wind shook the branches where they were sitting. The sky darkened as gray clouds streaked across the sun.

"Guys, we better head home, quick," Jeff yelled. "Look at the lake. It's getting rough!"

David was pointing. "Wait! Over there. Hillside School. See the window, up by the roof?"

Claire and Jeff focused their binoculars. A light was shining from the attic.

"Maybe it's sunlight reflecting off the glass," Jeff suggested. As the oldest, he tried to be logical and calm, as his father had been.

"No way," said Claire. "Clouds are hiding the sun. I think someone . . . someone's in Nettie's room!"

David said, "But isn't it sealed off? That's what Mr. Wellback said, and so did the old newspaper."

"Then why is a light on?"

The cousins kept looking. When they saw the shape of something moving inside the locked-up room, their hearts started beating fast. They swallowed, then, without a word, began scrambling down the tree.

7
Rainy Night

Claire hung on to the dogs' collars as Jeff and David paddled the canoe through the choppy water. Their arms and faces were wet from windblown spray. They were still too nervous to talk about what they had seen from the lookout tower. When at last the boat bumped against the dock, they were shivering with cold.

There was just enough time to put away the oars and life vests, then hurry inside to dry off. Just as they were zipping into warm jackets, Uncle Wyatt drove up in his Jeep. As usual he was wearing his cowboy hat.

"Hi, Daddy!" Claire said when they crowded into the backseat with the dogs and their backpacks.

"Hey, Uncle Wyatt," said the boys. "Thanks for picking us up."

"How'd the leaf raking go?" he asked them.

There was the clicking and snapping of seat belts. "Well" — Jeff cleared his throat — "we still have a lot to do, that's for sure."

They reached the café just as it started to rain. There was the good smell of dinner and freshly baked pies. Always friendly, Aunt Lilly greeted the children with hugs, then showed them to the corner booth. She had her daughter's red hair and green eyes.

"Boys, your mom will be here in a minute," she said about her sister. "And Gus, too." Gus Penny was Mr. Wellback's real name. He often joined the two families for meals.

While a waitress took care of the other diners, the Poseys, Bridgers, and Mr. Wellback sat down to meat loaf with roasted potatoes, salad, and applesauce. They passed around a basket of warm rolls.

"I'm on duty tonight," Dr. Bridger told her sons. "Aunt Lilly and Uncle Wyatt are also working late. So, after dinner would you kids rather rent some movies and go home, or stay in town for a few hours? The Lodge is showing a film on mountain climbing. Or there's the Harvest Festival in the community center. Just be back here by nine."

Jeff, David, and Claire kicked one another under the table. In the Jeep they had whispered their plans. They knew what they wanted to do.

"We'll stay in town," Jeff answered for the three of them.

Mr. Wellback looked at the cousins over the top of his spectacles. "You rascals are welcome to join me at the library for a school board meeting. We're trying to raise at least one million dollars to fix the roof at Hillside and other problems. Otherwise we'll have to sell to developers. Those city boys have stirred up quite a kerfuffle —"

Claire raised her hand. "Excuse me, what's —"

"— an uproar, young lady. *Kerfuffle* means uproar. It was my school, too. We old-timers like our history. But mostly we don't want to bus you scallywags out of town."

"Gus, we're grateful that you're standing in for us," said Uncle Wyatt.

Mr. Wellback nodded at Uncle Wyatt. Then the old man turned his attention to the dessert counter. "May we have some of Lilly's blue-berry cobbler tonight?"

The cousins reached the schoolhouse steps, out of breath from running with their dogs from the café. They brushed the rain from their sleeves. Jeff tried the tall, wooden door.

"Locked. Let's check around back."

With their flashlights, they crept alongside

the stone wall to stay dry until they came to a wide overhang. Long ago, this had been the Tuttles' carriage entrance where horses could stand out of the rain and snow. The children touched the door. To their surprise, it gave a loud groan and — ever so slowly — it swung open.

Yum-Yum and Rascal trotted inside as if they knew the place, followed by old Tessie. Jeff carefully latched the door behind them. It was pitch-dark, except for their beams of light swinging here and there. To the left were bumpy shadows of a narrow, steep stairway.

"Think we can find Nettie's room from here?" David called over his shoulder as he climbed two steps at a time, the dogs leading the way.

"David, wait! Let's stick together in case someone really is up there. Remember what happened to Mr. Wellback's friend?" Jeff peered into the shadows, trying to see the light from his younger brother, but David was already far ahead.

"Where *is* he?" Claire asked.

The floor creaked beneath their slow steps as they continued upward. The stairwell was frigid and they could feel a cold draft coming from a broken window.

"David?" they called.

But there was no answer.

8

An Old Secret

The stairway seemed steeper and more narrow as Claire and Jeff followed its upward twists and turns. When they came to the second landing, their flashlights fell upon a long hallway.

"Jeff, is this the music wing?" Claire asked.

"Looks like it. We must've come up the back stairs."

When they rounded a corner, they saw Tessie pacing in front of a door that was slightly ajar. She was whining and pawing at the wood, but the door wouldn't budge.

"What is it, girl?" Jeff asked, petting her. He shone his light into the opening. "Claire, it's the storeroom! The little dogs must've squeezed through. David? You in here?"

Jeff and Claire pushed the warped door until it scraped open.

"David?"

"Over here!" He waved his flashlight from behind a stack of old wooden chairs.

"What are you *doing*? We're supposed to stay together!"

"I'm sorry, Jeff. But Rascal and Yum-Yum went crazy, like they were chasing a squirrel or something. I had to find them. Check this out. It's what Claire wanted to see." The younger boy was shining his light on a painting. It hung on the wall, dusty and crooked.

When Claire saw the girl with dark braided hair, she cried, "That's the one! She was watching us through the window."

"Really?" Jeff asked.

Claire nodded. "It was Nettie all right." She hugged Yum-Yum to her chest for warmth. The room was so cold she could see her breath.

"So there *is* a ghost," said David, "and she's haunting our school. Now what?"

Jeff pointed his light up at the cobwebs. They swayed from wind coming in through a crack in the wall. "I don't know," he answered. "Hey . . . smell that? Like someone's baking a cake again."

"Sure do," said David. "And you know what else? A few minutes ago I heard that same piano music, but it stopped when I got in here. Just like yesterday."

Claire had recovered from her shock. With her flashlight, she studied the large painting. The girl was wearing an old-fashioned dress and high-buttoned shoes. A horse and buggy were in the background. A small plaque read: ANNETTE TUTTLE ~ SPRING, 1918.

"This must've been painted a few months before Nettie caught the flu." Claire touched the frame, trying to straighten it. But when she did, an icy draft rushed at them, as if from a tunnel.

The children stared in surprise. Before them was an opening in the wall that had been hidden behind the artwork. They lifted the painting and set it on the floor, then peered into the hole. Their flashlights revealed more cobwebs and another dark stairway going up.

In hushed voices they said, "*The secret passageway!*"

Claire turned to Jeff and David. Their faces were dark in shadow. "I'll go up if you go up."

"But isn't this where Mr. Wellback's friend fell?" Jeff wondered.

The cousins were quiet.

In a soft voice, Claire said, "We'll be careful. Right, David?"

"Right!"

The older boy looked at the glowing dial of

his watch. "I don't know, guys. It's after eight o'clock. If we're not back by nine, Uncle Wyatt and Aunt Lilly will worry about us exploring. Then they'll tell Mom. And with *all* of them worrying, we might never be able to solve this mystery."

"Well, how about if we're real quick?" David suggested.

Jeff took a deep breath. "Okay," he said. "Ten minutes. We've gotta be back here in *ten* minutes."

The children ducked into the passageway, following the yellow beams of their flash-lights up and up and up the stairs, David in the lead. But no sooner had the younger boy turned a dark corner than there was a frighten-ing *crunch*.

Claire stopped. "Did you hear that?" she whispered.

Jeff listened to the darkness. They could hear a muffled cry. It seemed far away.

"Is that —"

"Help!" someone cried.

9
Danger

"Help!" the voice cried again. "Hurry!"

"Oh, no . . . it's David," said Claire. "Do you think he —"

"I sure hope not," Jeff answered.

They swept their lights side to side. The narrow stairway was so steep, it was like climbing a ladder.

"Help!"

"We're coming!" Claire and Jeff yelled.

Around a corner they found their dogs

whining and worrying over a hole in the floor. All they could see of David were his hands clinging to a broken step. He was trying to pull himself up through the rotten wood where he had fallen. Four stories below him were the stones of a damp basement. His legs dangled in midair.

"Guys, hurry, I'm slipping!"

"Hang on!" Jeff cried. He and Claire dropped their flashlights and each grabbed one of David's arms. But the sleeve of David's jacket ripped away from Claire's grasp.

"Agghh!" David cried when he felt her let go. "I'm gonna fall!"

"I got you, buddy," Jeff said. "Try again, Claire."

This time she clutched David's shirt. Together, she and Jeff pulled and pulled until

David's elbows could rest on the step. Then Jeff dragged his brother up by the seat of his pants until he was safe on the stairway.

David was hunched over, his hand on his racing heart. He was trying to catch his breath.

"Are you okay?" Jeff asked, ruffling his brother's hair.

"I think so. *Whew*, you guys found me just in time. I didn't see the hole until my leg went through. It freaks me out to think one of the dogs could've fallen. And Mr. Wellback's friend —"

"David, you're bleeding." Claire pointed to his scraped arms. Then she rummaged in her pack for the first-aid kit. "Hold still so I —"

Bam! A loud noise came from downstairs.

"What . . . was . . . that?"

They listened. They could hear the wind outside, but nothing else.

"Sounded like a door slammed," David whispered. "What if we're locked in this place?"

Claire shone her light down the steep stairs. "Well, we can't stay here forever," she said. "And look, the dogs aren't nervous. Let's keep going."

The children made their way back down to the storeroom. They rehung the painting — making sure it was straight and hid the hole in the wall — and crept through the maze of furniture. The warped door was still ajar.

David said, "This thing hasn't budged. That noise must've been the door where we came in."

"But I closed it tight," Jeff insisted, "and latched it. The only way it could've slammed shut is if someone . . . if someone opened it. Are we being followed?"

Claire thought a moment. "Maybe it was the janitor going home for the day."

"Then why did I hear piano music before?" David asked. "And remember, we smelled a spicy cake again?"

The cousins pondered these things while Claire cleaned David's scrapes with gauze and Bactine, as her mother had taught her. Jeff held a flashlight so she could see. With her tweezers, she was able to pull some splinters from David's bloody arm. He was so relieved he hadn't fallen to the basement, he didn't complain that Claire's Band-Aids were decorated with pink flowers.

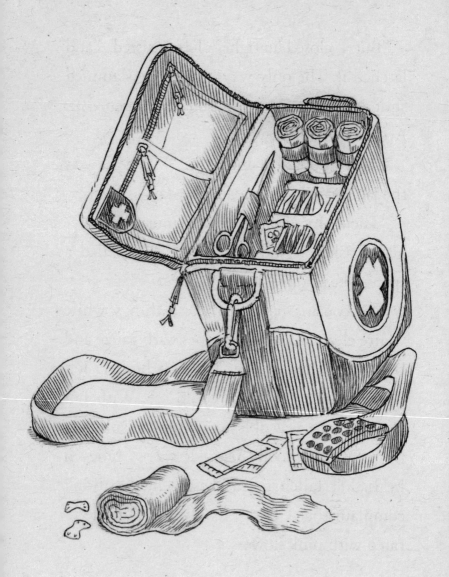

*   *   *

It was snowing when the children left the dark schoolhouse. A streetlight revealed footprints in the new snow.

"Someone *was* here!" David exclaimed. "Ghosts don't wear shoes or slam doors."

They bent down to study the tracks. They remembered their father teaching them how to read fresh snowfall for signs of animals or humans.

"Weird," said Jeff. "There's no tread. Can't tell if they're from boots or sneakers. But this person was running. See how far apart the feet are, one in front of the other?"

"And it was only a few minutes ago," David added. "Snowflakes haven't covered 'em up yet. I wonder who it was?"

Jeff checked his watch. "We're in luck. It's only eight-thirty. The tracks lead straight to town, so we have time to follow them. Let's go!"

Because it was Saturday night, the stores were open late. The cousins followed the prints past the bookstore and pharmacy, past the bakery, a jeweler, then the library. Next door to the hardware store was the new antique shop, but there were so many footprints along that part of the sidewalk, the cousins couldn't see where the running person had gone.

"We lost him!" David said. "Now what?"

"Hey, guys, check this out." Claire was looking in the window of Grace's Antiques, at a toy train set. The locomotive was chugging along tracks that circled a display of old dollhouses, past miniature streetlamps. "Okay if we go in for a minute?" she asked. "The café's just around the corner, so we won't be late."

The brothers sighed, frustrated about the mysterious footprints. "Okay," they said.

The children leashed their dogs to a bench. When they entered the shop, a tiny bell jingled against the door. "Hello," Claire said to the owners, Mr. and Mrs. Garcia, who were new to Cabin Creek. "May we look at the trains?"

"Please, be our guests," the man answered.

"It smells good in here, like a bakery," David said.

"Why, thank you. Along with antiques, we sell wind chimes and scented candles," said the woman. "They make nice gifts. They're very homey."

Jeff went over to a shelf were there were some fossils of ancient bugs. He liked prehistoric things. As he was examining them, he noticed a stout red candle burning there. "Mm . . . this one smells like cinnamon gummy bears."

"We also have pumpkin pie candles," said Mr. Garcia. "Lemon zest, vanilla pudding, spice cake, you name it."

At the mention of spice cake, the kids exchanged looks. "Do you have any that smell like . . . gingerbread?" Claire asked.

"Oh, yes," answered Mrs. Garcia. "We've only been open for one week, but so far that is our most popular candle. It seems that everyone in Cabin Creek loves the aroma of gingerbread."

10

Another Fright

After saying good-bye to Mr. and Mrs. Garcia, the cousins hurried outside and around the snowy corner. They walked into the café at nine o'clock sharp.

While waiting for Aunt Lilly to close out the cash register, they sat at a table with cups of hot cocoa. David opened his sketchbook and began writing a new list of clues.

"Number One," Claire dictated to him. "A scented candle. I bet someone at school has one that smells like cinnamon or gingerbread. And since the antique store is new, maybe the person just bought it. That's why we never noticed an aroma until now. At least, that's my theory."

"But who?" Jeff wondered. "It must be someone who doesn't care about the fire hazard. And how come we only smell cinnamon — or whatever it is — when there's piano music?"

"Piano music coming from *nowhere*," David reminded them. "That's Number Two."

"Number Three," said Claire. "A slammed door and footprints of someone running away from the schoolhouse."

"Don't forget Number Four," Jeff added. "Remember from the lookout tower, how we saw a light in the school attic and something moving?"

"Number Five," said David, writing quickly with his pencil. "The painting of Nettie Tuttle looks like the girl Claire saw at the window. Sure seems like a ghost is playing tricks on us."

Claire leaned over the table so the boys could hear her whisper. "I bet the secret passageway has more clues. We *have* to go back, okay? *Tomorrow*."

"*Tomorrow*," the brothers whispered.

But Sunday turned out to be a family day at home. The dusting of snow had melted, so the children finished raking leaves in their yards. They helped Uncle Wyatt carry the canoe, rowboat, and paddles to the shed, to store for winter. Later they helped Mr.

Wellback stack firewood on his cabin porch, then invited him to supper. Not until the dishes were done that evening did the cousins finally settle at the Bridger table to do their homework.

The next day after school, Jeff and David were learning origami in their art class. They were supposed to be folding their colored sheets of paper into pretty ornaments to sell at the school fundraiser. But instead, the brothers were making paper airplanes.

David launched one of his with a flick of his wrist. It soared up to the ceiling, circled, then made a gentle landing on the windowsill — the very window where outside, a face was now looking in at them. The brothers blinked and stared, but the face vanished. They jumped up from their table.

"Bridger boys!" called Miss Wiggins before they had taken one step. "Back in your seats, please. You can do all the walking around you want when class is over."

Five long minutes later, Miss Wiggins rang the little brass bell on her desk, excusing everyone for the day. Jeff and David ran down the hall to pick up Claire at her flute lesson. While explaining to her what they'd just seen, the three put on their sweaters and rushed out into the cold afternoon air.

"Over here," Jeff said, running down the steps. He led them to the bushes below the art room window. "Let's look for footprints."

It took only a moment for Claire to shout her discovery. The brothers peered over her shoulder.

The melted snow had left mud below the

shrubbery, where there were several strange prints. All were the size of a teacup, about two feet apart.

"This reminds me of Dad's ladder," said Jeff. "Remember last year when he put up Christmas lights? Guys, I'm sure someone was here a few minutes ago. See, the prints are fresh."

David set a piece of his notebook paper on the ground. With his thumb he measured the shapes, then drew them in his notebook. He labeled them *Number Six: A ladder for spying on the art room, but where did it go?"*

"Let's keep looking," Jeff suggested. "If we find it, maybe there'll be more clues."

They walked around the schoolhouse until they came to a gravel path. It led to a grove of pine trees where there was a large shed.

Claire said, "I've seen the gardener put stuff in there. Let's look, but quick. I'm getting cold."

The cousins hurried over to the trees. The shed door was just like Uncle Wyatt's garage, with the handle on the bottom. A padlock dangled there, unlocked. When Claire tugged at the handle, the door opened easily, sliding up and overhead. They took their flashlights from their packs and peered inside. There were rakes, shovels, coils of garden hoses, and bags of potting soil. The largest item was a riding lawn mower with a tall seat. And hanging lengthwise against one of the walls was an aluminum ladder.

"Here it is!" cried Jeff.

David held his drawing against the

bottom stubs of the ladder, which were caked with mud.

"Perfect fit!" he cried. "And the dirt is still wet, so it's fresh. Now, to find out who was using it and what for."

A shuffling noise came from outside. The cousins turned just in time to see someone in a blue parka reach up for the door handle and roll it shut with a slam.

Click went the padlock.

11

Locked In

The children rushed to the door. They tried to lift it, but it was locked from the outside. They banged on it and kicked.

"Let us out!"

They heard footsteps of someone running away.

"We're all alone," Claire whispered.

"Stay calm, guys," said Jeff. "Somebody's just trying to scare us."

"Well, it worked!" she cried. "This is a terrible kerfuffle! I don't like it in here!"

"Me, neither," said David.

They shone their flashlights around the dark shed, looking for something to pry open the door. Shadows wiggled along the walls like odd creatures. The air felt colder by the minute.

Again, the children yelled and pounded on the door, hoping someone would hear them. They listened. The only sound was their breathing.

David took his walkie-talkie from his pack. "I've had it! Time to call Uncle Wyatt —"

"Wait a sec, David." Jeff felt his courage returning. "If we call Uncle Wyatt for help, he'll definitely tell Mom. They'll probably report this to the principal and then —"

"— and then," Claire added, now also feeling brave, "it'll mess up our investigation."

"Oh, yeah," said David. "I almost forgot."

"So now," Jeff said, "let's figure this out while we're looking around. Who wants to scare us?"

"Those developers," was David's quick answer. He'd been pondering this all weekend. "They want us to think the school is haunted so we'll tell our parents. Then our parents will tell the school board, then *everyone* will be scared and agree to sell. That way the developers can tear down Hillside, build condos, and make tons of money."

Claire said, "Don't forget Rex and Ronald McCoy. They want to go to the new school in Fairfield because of the candy machines. Also they think there's no homework. That's just dumb. School always has homework."

"I still can't figure out the face in the window," said David. "Or the piano or the spicy cake smell."

"Same here," Jeff replied. "Except maybe someone is sneaking around the school with a candle from Grace's Antiques."

"That seems like something the McCoy boys would do," Claire said. "They don't care about rules or safety. I bet the developers are paying them to scare people."

"Right!" David agreed. He had climbed onto the lawn mower seat and was pretending to drive. "I think we should rev this thing up and bust outta here, right through the wall!"

Jeff was giving the mower a good look with his flashlight. He walked around it, studying the ground.

"Guys, I think I found a way out of here." Jeff showed them the muddy tire tracks in front *and* behind the mower. "Looks like the gardener drives this in through *that* door — where we came in — then *out* through here."

He shone his light against the back wall. There was a thin crack down the middle, from top to bottom. Touching it, he could feel cold air.

"It's a double door!" Jeff said. "See, there's a latch up high, holding the two sides together." He stood on a toolbox to unlock it, but the door only rattled. It didn't open.

Claire knelt on the dirt floor. "Here's another latch!" she cried. "But there's stuff in front of it."

Together, the three children pushed aside some hoses and bags of soil to reach the bottom lock.

At last, the doors swung wide open like a pair of arms, and the cousins ran out into the frosty air. Late afternoon light was slanting through the woods. They ran to their bikes and rode home as the sun was setting, arriving just in time for dinner.

In painting class the next day, Claire heard the mysterious but gentle music of Mozart's minuet. Once again, it was coming from the heater grate. She gave Jeff and David a knowing smile and they nodded in return. Miss Wiggins stopped for a moment to listen, also smiling.

A baking aroma drifted into the art room, but the cousins seemed to be the only ones who noticed. They tidied up their easels, then washed their paintbrushes at the sink. When Miss Wiggins rang her little bell to dismiss class, they got their backpacks and calmly left the room.

This time, the cousins had a plan.

12

An Astonishing Sight

The music wing was lively with students practicing their instruments. Many were planning to perform solos or duets at the fundraiser. Everyone was trying to earn money to save Hillside School from being sold to the developers.

At Room Twelve, the cousins could still hear the Mozart minuet. Ever so carefully, they pushed open the door so it wouldn't scrape the floor, then quietly closed it behind them. This time the mysterious music didn't stop. It kept playing. They flicked on their flashlights.

The warped piano was as silent and dusty as before. However, the portrait of Nettie Tuttle was crooked again. Someone or *something* had moved it.

From the eerie shadows, the children gave one another nervous glances. They opened their backpacks to put on knit caps and sweaters, so they would be warm. Then Jeff took out a flat board they had found in Uncle Wyatt's shed. It was two feet long, long enough to cover the broken step. David had a tube of superglue and several shims — thin pieces of wood — that could help wedge the board between the walls after being glued. It would be a bumpy repair, but at least no one else would fall through.

Without speaking, the cousins then lifted the painting from the wall and ducked into the cold passageway. They crept up the stairs, their lights aimed in front of them to avoid any broken wood.

But when they came to where David had fallen, the step had been covered with a metal cooking pan.

Claire bent down to look. "*Someone's been here*," she said.

They stared at the pan. Then Jeff nudged it. It wobbled, exposing the gaping hole. "It's still dangerous," he said. "Claire, shine your light while David and I glue down our board.

Whoever put this here didn't know about fixing things."

As the cousins continued upward, the music grew louder. And the aroma of sweet spice grew stronger. Finally, they came to a small door.

"Ready?" Jeff whispered.

"Ready."

Jeff turned the knob, pushing the door open to the attic. Their flashlights revealed an eerie scene.

"*Wow*," said Claire. "This must have been Nettie's room."

Frilly curtains were at the window. A canopy bed was covered with a patchwork quilt.

On the pillow was a porcelain doll in a lacy dress and tiny black boots. The doll was sitting up straight with a doll smile, as if Nettie had just put her there and run outside to play. Beside the bed was a small three-legged table. On it was a Bible and a kerosene lamp. It was unlit, but its glass chimney was shiny clean.

A baby carriage in the corner had several teddy bears dressed up in bonnets and bows.

Claire whispered, "The roof hasn't leaked up here and it's not dusty. It's perfect, like a museum."

"A *girl's* museum," said Jeff. "Yuck."

"I bet this is where she died," David said. He took out his notebook and quickly sketched the bedside table. Just for fun he drew the doll with wild frizzy hair and frizzy eyebrows.

The cousins stared at the antique toys and furniture. They tried to imagine the young girl who had gone to Lost Island with her brothers so long ago.

A tinkling of piano keys came from another room. They turned their flashlights off so they wouldn't be seen, then ducked into a low hallway. A curtain hung at the end of the dark hall. It rippled in the draft, revealing a light up ahead.

The children tiptoed until they could peek behind the curtain. Before them was a cupola, a tower-like room with windows on five sides. It was empty except for an extraordinary sight:

A young girl was playing a piano. She had

brown hair in two long braids and was wearing an old-fashioned dress and high-buttoned boots.

The cousins were too astonished to move.

"*Nettie?*" they whispered. "*Nettie Tuttle?*"

13

More Questions
than Ever

The girl at the piano was playing Mozart's Minuet in D major.

"*Nettie?*" the cousins whispered again.

The girl didn't respond. Her hands seemed to float over the keys as the music continued.

"It's a ghost," David whispered. "It can't hear us."

"I'm going to see if it has a face," said Claire. She edged along one of the walls for a closer look. The room was warm from candles that smelled like gingerbread.

Suddenly, the girl jumped off the stool, her hand over her mouth. "You scared me!" she cried.

Claire stepped forward. "It's you! I saw you looking in the upstairs window."

"Please don't tell anyone I'm here. I'll get in trouble."

Now the boys came from behind the curtain. David touched the girl's shoulder. "You're not a ghost. Who are you?"

"My name is Sophie."

"Boy, do we have a lot of questions for you!" Jeff exclaimed.

"Do we ever!" said David.

Though the cousins were shocked to see this peculiar girl, they didn't forget their manners. They introduced themselves. Then they noticed the beautiful view. They could see the town of Cabin Creek and the surrounding forests. Blue Mountain Lodge looked pretty next to the Marina and sparkling lake. Lost Island was in the distance, hidden behind a peninsula except for the very tip-top of its tallest tree — where the cousins had climbed with their binoculars a few days earlier.

Turning back to Sophie, David said, "When we were in our lookout tower, we saw this room. A light was on. Have you been up here?"

"Yes," she answered. "I've been coming every day for about a week. It's a long story, but we just moved here from River Valley —"

"You just moved here?" Jeff asked. He

picked up one of the red candles. "We saw some of these in Grace's Antiques. The man and lady said the store opened a week ago. Are you — ?"

"They're my parents. I'm Sophie Garcia. I bring candles to warm up the room."

David crossed his arms with a *harrumph*. "Well, that explains all those good smells. But why do you sneak up here in the first place? Candles can cause a fire, you know — and how come you aren't in school?"

"And why are you dressed like that painting downstairs?" Claire asked. "No offense, but you look like you're from *Little House on the Prairie*."

"I know," Sophie replied. "See, we had two moving vans. One was full of antiques and old-time costumes for the store. The other has the stuff for our house — our furniture, my school clothes, my piano. I really miss my piano. Anyway, *that* van broke down in the desert and is being fixed. When we drove to Cabin Creek, I was wearing sweatpants and a sweatshirt — that's all I have with me. So when Mom puts them in the laundry, she lets me borrow this outfit from the store. I wear her coat over it to go outside. It's totally embarrassing."

Sophie looked down at her long skirt. "I'm in third grade. No way will I go to class wearing *this*, or sweatpants, or pajamas. And since we don't have money to buy extra clothes, Mom and Dad said I don't have to start school until our van gets here. They gave me workbooks for keeping up. After I read for an hour, I get to explore town on my bike. But

they would worry if they knew I'm up here alone."

Claire liked the bravery of this new girl. "Your secret is safe with us," she said. From her backpack she took out a bar of chocolate. She broke it into pieces to share, then passed around her canteen.

"Hey, thanks," said Sophie. "I'm starved."

Jeff was thinking. "*So* . . . were you here the other night when it was snowing?"

"Yeah. I heard noises downstairs, so I was as quiet as possible. I blew out the candles. It was freaky going down in the dark. When I got to the junk room, two little dogs were there, so I hid —"

"Rascal and Yum-Yum!" said David. "So that's why they went bonkers. You're the one who slammed the door and ran to town."

Sophie looked at the cousins quizzically. "*You* were here? I thought it was the janitor. He leaves the back door unlocked. I didn't want him to see me because he already yelled at me for being on his ladder. He said it was dangerous and he hurried away with it. I was just trying to see what a classroom looked like, without kids laughing at my clothes. I promised him I'd never do it again. And I haven't —"

"Wait a second," David interrupted. "You only climbed the ladder once?"

"Yep."

"But we saw a face in the window *yesterday*," Jeff said. "The ladder even left prints in the mud."

"Well, it wasn't me. I promised the janitor I wouldn't."

"Then after that, someone locked us in a shed," Claire added. "We still don't know who, or how come."

Sophie's brown eyes were kind. "I would *never* do anything like that."

"Are you the one who put a pan on that broken step?" David asked her.

"Yes. Just to cover up the hole. I'm glad you guys didn't fall in."

Even though the cousins had just met Sophie Garcia, they believed she was telling the truth. But now they had more questions than ever.

14

Some Answers

The four children sat on the floor of the cupola, warmed by the candles. While they shared another chocolate bar, the cousins described everything they had learned about Nettie Tuttle. They also told about the men trying to buy the building.

"Oh, I hope Hillside School isn't torn down," Sophie said. "I really like it here. It's cozy. You guys would hate the one in Fairfield."

"How do you know?" Jeff asked.

"That's where I went before," she replied. "All the kids from River Valley are bused there. It's humongous. I have two baby brothers and that's why my parents moved their antique store up here. They love the mountains. And they want us to grow up in a small town."

"What about the candy machines and no homework?" Claire wanted to know.

Sophie laughed. "Oh, there's homework all right. It's the high school that has soda and candy machines in the halls. My parents were really mad about that. They say schools shouldn't make money by selling junk food to kids."

"Sorry to change the subject," David said, "but there's still a puzzle we haven't solved." He had opened his sketchbook to their list of clues. "Remember what Mr. Wellback told us? How when he was a kid, he and his friends heard mysterious music?"

"Right," Claire said. "It was only once in a while. Also, sometimes they saw an odd little man with an odd little bag, sneaking through the woods behind school."

"But they never knew who the man was," Jeff continued, "or what he was doing. Sorta like us trying to figure out the guy who locked us in the shed."

"This town sure has a lot of mysteries," said Sophie.

"You're not kidding!"

"Is this your first time up in this room?" Sophie asked the cousins.

"Yep," said David. "And we've lived here our whole lives. How'd *you* find it?"

Sophie fiddled with one of her braids, looking thoughtful. Then she smiled.

"I like exploring. My first day, I found the music wing. The doors to all those little rooms have windows, except one. I wondered why, so I opened it and snuck inside with my flashlight. You know the painting of that girl? It was crooked. When I tried to fix it, I felt a breeze —"

"From the secret passageway!" Claire cried.

"Yeah, it's secret all right. All those cobwebs, and more stairs. I thought *oh, cool, maybe there's a skeleton or treasure up there.*"

"But what about that hole in the floor?" David asked. "How'd you keep from falling?"

"I was going super slow," Sophie replied. "When I saw it, I started counting steps. I counted going up and going down. That way

I always knew where it was. So that's how I discovered this place."

"You like solving mysteries, too!" Claire exclaimed.

"Oh, yes," she answered. "My dad calls me Sophie the Sleuth."

"And you're good on the piano," Jeff said.

"Thank you. I couldn't believe this one sounds so pretty. It's really weird for an old piano not to be out of tune. Anyway, that's why I kept coming up here, to practice. Also, I like looking out the windows at town and the lake and all the kids coming and going. I can't wait to start school for real."

David sketched a map in his notebook. On the top he wrote, FOR SOPHIE THE SLEUTH. "Here's how you get to our cabin from town," he told her, tearing out the paper. "Our mom loves having company. We'll ask if our families can have supper together. We can talk about the fundraiser. It's next weekend."

"How much money does our school need?" asked Sophie.

The cousins smiled. Sophie had said *our* school. She was definitely their friend.

"To fix everything up?" Claire gave a casual shrug. "Oh, about a ga-zillion dollars."

Sophie started blowing out her candles. "Let's go. There's something I have to show you guys."

15

Sophie the Sleuth

The children gathered the snuffed candles, then put them in Sophie's pack. By flashlight, they hurried from the cupola, downstairs, and outside.

"First, let's ride to my parents' shop," Sophie said.

While they were unlocking their bikes, Jeff glanced toward the woods where the shed was sheltered. The double doors were open and a teenage boy was carrying out a ladder over his shoulder. He was wearing a striped ski cap, mittens, and a parka. A blue parka.

"*It's Rex McCoy,*" Jeff whispered.

The cousins marched over to the teenager. Sophie stayed by the bike rack, embarrassed by her long dress.

"Whoa," Rex said, when the three approached him.

"What are you doing with this ladder?" Jeff asked.

"Huh?"

"Are the developers paying you to scare us?"

"What're you babies talking about? I'm cleaning leaves from the gutters of this crummy old school, what else? Some of us have jobs, you know."

"So it was *you* looking in the window yesterday," David said.

"Yeah. What about it?"

Claire pointed to the teenager's sleeve. "Someone in a blue parka locked us in the shed yesterday. Was it you?"

Rex set the ladder on the ground. "I came right back to let you out, but you had already flown the coop. I was just teasing."

"You can't go around doing stuff like that," Jeff said. "It's not funny."

"Are you still trying to pay back your dad for his boat that you wrecked?" Claire asked.

"Yeah. It's taking forever."

"Well, if you wanna keep your job," said David, "you gotta stop playing stupid tricks."

Rex looked down at his feet. His shoulders

sagged. "I hate working. I wish I could be making paper airplanes like you guys. I'm sorry I scared you."

The cousins glanced at one another. They felt sad for the teenage boy who was always getting in trouble. "Okay," said Jeff. "We'll see you later. We've got things to do."

The path to town went through the woods. Sophie led the way, but suddenly she skidded to a stop and jumped off her bike. She held a finger over her lips, for the cousins to be quiet. Then she motioned for them to follow her.

They dragged their bikes under the boughs of a pine tree and crouched in the cold dirt. Through the branches, they could see a man creeping through the trees. He wore a hooded jacket that hid his face, and a backpack. Twice he stopped to look around as if he were listening.

The children didn't move. They watched him come closer and closer. When he came out of the woods onto the trail toward school, he passed their hiding place.

"*Shhh*," David said. But he shushed so loudly, the stranger heard him. He stopped and turned around.

Afraid to move, the children watched the man's shoes. Slowly, he walked toward them. Soon he was so close, they could read the Converse label on his sneakers.

"I know you're in there. Come out."

Still, the children didn't move.

"If you don't get out here by the count of ten, I'll drag you myself." When he ducked low to see under the tree, his hood fell away from his face.

The children were astonished to see a young woman with curly blond hair. She didn't look at all scary.

"So it's you!" the woman said to Sophie. "You've really messed things up for me. Come on, now, get out from there. What're you kids doing, hiding in the woods? It's getting dark."

The children pulled their bikes from under the branches. Jeff said, "You made us nervous. You weren't on the path like normal people."

"We should report you for sneaking around our school," David said.

"And who *are* you?" Sophie asked. "What do you mean, I've messed things up?"

The woman took a deep breath and looked

skyward, as if trying to be patient. "I'm a piano tuner," she said. "I've been trying to do my job, but you" — she pointed to Sophie — "have been up in the attic this past week. Every time I went up those stairs, there you were. I should've just chased you away, but I'm not supposed to make any ruckus."

"So you've been tuning Nettie's piano?" Claire asked.

"Twice a year," she answered. "Ever since I graduated from music school. It used to be my grandfather's job. A super-rich family from long ago left money for that piano to stay tuned and for the furniture up there to be dusted. It's a secret. Only me, the janitor, and some lawyers know about it."

"If it's a secret, why are you telling us?" asked Jeff.

The young woman shifted the pack on her back. It rattled with her tools. "People will find out in a couple weeks anyway. Everyone knows the school's going to be torn down. This is probably the last time I tune that thing before it goes to a museum. Well, I've gotta get to work. You kids should let your parents know where you are."

16

A Final Surprise

Sophie and the cousins parked their bikes in front of Grace's Antiques and went inside. The shop had the good aroma of flickering cinnamon and gingerbread candles. The miniature train click-clacked along its tracks in the window display, and Christmas carols played softly from a radio.

"Mom, it's exactly like this one," said Sophie, pointing to a color photo in a book. "See, David drew a picture of it."

David showed his sketch of the bedside table.

"*Whew*," Mr. Garcia whistled. "From your description, Sophie, and from this drawing, young man, I'd say this is a Pre-Revolutionary War tea table, from Philadelphia."

"That's a long name. What does it mean?" asked Claire.

"It means," said Mr. Garcia, removing his glasses, "that it's more than two hundred years old. Before the American Revolution. If it's what I think it is, this dainty three-legged table is worth a fortune."

"What kind of fortune?"

Mr. Garcia gave the children a serious look. "For the moment we'll forget you kids were in the attic without permission. But this little tea table could be worth, oh, between one hundred and fifty thousand dollars up to several million dollars."

"What!" David cried. "Several million bucks?"

"Depends on its condition," Mr. Garcia went on. "My guess is — because the attic has been untouched all these years — we're looking at a table of great historic value. Benjamin Franklin or George Washington may have had their afternoon tea served to them on this."

Claire stretched onto her tiptoes with excitement. "A ga-zillion dollars is just what our school needs."

"Now, don't count your chickens before the eggs are hatched," said Mrs. Garcia. She, too, had brown hair and gentle eyes. "We'll inspect the table, then go talk to the school board. But from what the piano tuner told us, everything in the attic is to stay as it was in 1918."

"That's right," said her husband. "We heard that nothing in the attic is ever to be moved. Or sold."

Three days later, Mr. Wellback stood at the front of the meeting hall. His white hair and white beard were trim from a visit to the barber. He held up his hand for quiet.

"Thanks for coming to our school fundraiser," he said in his deep voice, which silenced the crowd of families and townsfolk. "We'll start with a clarinet solo in just a moment. First, an announcement."

Jeff, David, Claire, and Sophie sat in the front row, eager to hear Mr. Wellback's news. Sophie was spiffed up in a pair of jeans, purple sneakers, and a red sweater Claire had given her from her closet. Both girls had brushed their hair into ponytails and wore sparkly headbands.

"Some of you know about the Tuttle family," Mr. Wellback began. "They donated their mansion to be used as a school, back in 1918. No-way-no-how was anything in the attic to be disturbed. Well, our lawyers have been reading those old documents and found some good news for us."

Claire raised her hand to ask what the good news was, but Mr. Wellback just winked at her.

"There's a special clause," he continued. "It says that if ever the mansion is in danger of being torn down, the school board has permission to sell Nettie's piano and other belongings. But only if the money will save the building. Since the stairway is so narrow, the Tuttles used pulleys and such to lift Nettie's furniture from the lawn up through a window. We'll do the same to get everything out."

Mr. and Mrs. Garcia went up to the front and stood next to Mr. Wellback. They introduced themselves. "We're new to Cabin Creek and are eager to meet everyone. After the music program, please visit our booth. We'll be selling candles and wind chimes to help the school fund."

Then Mr. Garcia explained that Nettie's little tea table was worth nearly two million dollars. At first the crowd was silent. Then there was a murmur of voices.

Two million dollars? people were asking one another. Finally, as the good news sunk in, everyone erupted in cheers and applause.

"And that's not all," Mr. Wellback said, again waiting for the crowd to quiet. "As president of the Cabin Creek Historical Society, I am organizing an exhibit for the museum. We'll call it Nettie's Room. The first thing we'll do is replace the tea table with a look-alike, so everyone will know the story."

As adults murmured their approval, Mr. Wellback held up his hand one more time.

"Now, my favorite part," he said. "There's enough money to turn the attic into an observatory. We'll have telescopes. The sky is so clear up here in the mountains, children can study the stars and planets. I, myself, will teach the scallywags. Astronomy will be fun."

The audience broke into applause.

The cousins wiggled in their seats from all the good news. First off, they loved watching the stars at night. Second, Hillside wasn't haunted after all and it wasn't going to be turned into condos. Third, they would still be able to ride their bikes to school.

And best of all, they had a new friend who also liked to solve mysteries.

GET A SNEAK PEEK AT
JEFF, DAVID, AND CLAIRE'S
NEXT EXCITING ADVENTURE:

#5: THE BLIZZARD ON BLUE MOUNTAIN

The Blizzard
on Blue Mountain

Ten-year-old David Bridger dug in the pockets of his ski parka. He could feel coins, gum wrappers, and parts of a sandwich, but no key. His older brother, Jeff, stood beside him in the snow, worried. They were at the chalet, halfway up Blue Mountain. On weekends and during school breaks, the boys helped out in the cafeteria with their cousin, Claire Posey. In exchange, the three children received free lift tickets and a free lunch.

"Where else could you have put it?" Jeff asked. "We're going to be in so much trouble if you've lost another one."

"It was here a minute ago," David said. He glanced around the deck where skiers were having picnics and enjoying the sunshine. There was a pleasant aroma of wood smoke from an outdoor barbecue.

"I took the snow shovel back to the shed," David explained, "and unlocked the door. Then I set the key on the railing while I put things away. Same as last time."

Jeff was twelve and wanted to set a good example. He had brown hair and sensitive brown eyes. He showed his younger brother the string around his neck, which held an identical key: It, too, opened the shed and the cafeteria's back door. "See, this is how I keep mine safe. Miss Allen said she'll take away our ski passes if one more thing goes missing."

"I know, I *know*. Help me find it, please?"

The brothers retraced David's path from the shed to the cafeteria. They checked the lost and found. Again, they searched pockets. But there was no key.

"Now what?" David asked. His blue eyes looked worried. He yanked off his knit cap, revealing blond hair sticking every which way.

Jeff sighed. "I don't know. Let's think about this for a minute."

Beyond the sundeck was a control booth for the ski lift. The motor was loud. It clicked and groaned as it rolled the dangling chairs uphill like a giant pulley. The brothers looked longingly at the slope where the chairs continued to the top of the mountain.

They had hoped to go snowboarding with Claire after finishing their chores.

"I hate being in trouble," David said. He saw a french fry that a kid had dropped, and tossed it to some tiny birds pecking the ground — mountain chickadees. But a large gray jay who had been watching from a pine tree swooped down and snatched the fry. It flew away with it dangling from its beak like a worm.

"We're not supposed to feed wild animals!" called Claire from the cafeteria doorway. She was only nine, but she liked to supervise her older cousins. She had green eyes and red hair that she usually wore pulled back in a ponytail like today. A chef's apron was over her jeans and sweater. She went to the brothers with a concerned look.

"Guys, did you take a bag of potato chips from the kitchen?"

The boys looked at each other. "Huh?" they said.

She put her hand on her hip. "Don't tease me."

"Wasn't us, Claire. Sorry."

Just then Miss Allen marched across the deck. She wore dainty boots with fur around her ankles and skinny pants. "I need to have a word with you children," she said.

She showed them her wrist. Her sleeve was rolled up.

"My watch is missing," she said. "I took it off to scrub some dishes and set it on the windowsill. Now it's gone. This is the last straw. Since you're the only kids with keys to the kitchen, I'm holding you responsible. I'm taking your passes away."

If you love mystery, be sure to visit

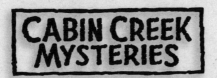

CABIN CREEK MYSTERIES

a small town with a lot of BIG secrets!

#1: THE SECRET OF ROBBER'S CAVE

#2: THE CLUE AT THE BOTTOM OF THE LAKE

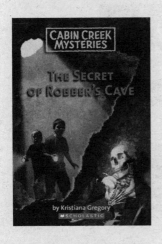

#3: The Legend of Skull Cliff

#5: The Blizzard on Blue Mountain